PRIMARY
WING FEATHER

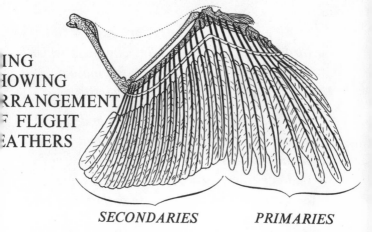

ING
HOWING
RRANGEMENT
F FLIGHT
EATHERS

SECONDARIES   *PRIMARIES*

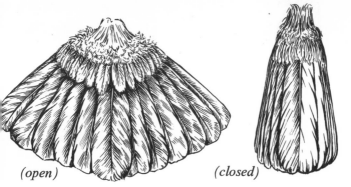

(open)   *(closed)*

ARRANGEMENT OF TAIL FEATHERS

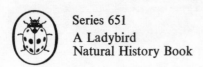

Series 651
A Ladybird
Natural History Book

Almost everyone has some interest in birds and bird life, and this is a book which will give pleasure and much fascinating information to readers of all ages.

With a simple and clear text and superb colour illustrations, it describes feathers and flight, beaks and bills, feet and legs, eyes and ears, nests, songs, food and defence against enemies, and rouses enthusiasm for further study.

BIRDS
and how they live

by
F. E. NEWING, B.Sc. *and* RICHARD BOWOOD

with illustrations by
RONALD LAMPITT

Publishers: Ladybird Books Ltd . Loughborough
© Ladybird Books Ltd (formerly Wills & Hepworth Ltd) 1966
Printed in England

THE BIRD KINGDOM

The true meaning of the word 'animal' is any creature which can move of its own free will, including birds, fishes, insects, reptiles, and mammals. We commonly mean all these when we use the word animals. Birds, then, are animals. They are different from the other animals because they are clothed with feathers, have two legs and two wings, and with some exceptions, possess the wonderful ability to fly.

Like every other living thing, birds have developed to suit their environment and their needs, through the extremely gradual process of evolution. At some distant time in the history of the world, hundreds of millions of years ago, cold-blooded reptiles changed gradually into warm-blooded flying animals. Scientists have certain clues to the mystery of this change.

One such clue is the skeleton of a prehistoric creature which was part reptile and part bird, called the Archaeopteryx (pronounced: *Ark-ay-opter-iks*). The picture shows what this strange creature might have looked like when it was alive millions of years ago. It was partly feathered and had wings with which it could perhaps fly, or glide.

From the Archaeopteryx, and other long extinct creatures, have developed the great variety of different birds whose habits, colours and song delight us.

4

7214 0124 4

ARCHAEOPTERYX
on a tree fern

FEATHERS

Besides being clothed with feathers, a bird has scales on its feet and legs. These scales are a link with the reptiles which were its very distant ancestors. The feathers serve to keep the body warm and to protect it from wet, and they are both light and strong to enable the bird to fly.

The colouring of feathers is important in providing protection from enemies, as described on page 46. Sometimes, as with the magpie, the colour forms a dazzle pattern which breaks up the appearance of the bird's shape.

Feathers play an important part at mating time when the male will make himself as splendid as possible by ruffling or displaying his feathers to impress a female. The peacock is a splendid example. Another use for feathers it to make a soft and cosy nest-lining for the benefit of newly-hatched birds.

Some birds are covered with soft fluffy feathers, or 'down', when they are hatched. Birds hatched in nests, and which start life quite naked, grow this down in a few days. As they grow up they develop pinions and flying feathers on wings and tail. The adult bird has both soft body feathers and strong flying feathers.

Worn feathers are discarded and new ones grown when a bird moults, which is at least once a year and sometimes twice. A bird looks after its feathers by preening them with its beak, using a special oil obtained from a gland at the base of the tail.

JAY
preening

Down-covered
chick of
domestic fowl

Newly-hatched
chick in
feather-lined nest

WINGS AND TAIL

A feather consists of a central quill from which grow the barbs making the 'vane' of the feather. The barbs have tiny hooks which fit into grooves in the next barb, thus making a single smooth surface. If you run your finger the wrong way along a feather, it will be ruffled; if you run it back again lightly the barbs will settle into position as the hooks fit into the grooves.

Wings have evolved over millions of years from forelimbs—the front legs or arms of early creatures. They are wonderfully designed for their main purpose, which is flight. Constructed of very strong but light feathers, wings can be folded back close to the body when the bird is at rest or walking or swimming, and can be extended for flying.

A wing has three principal kinds of feather. The longest, which grow on what would be the 'hand', are the *primaries*. Over these, and growing on the 'arm', are the *secondaries*. The *wing coverts* are shorter feathers over and under the long feathers.

The strong feathers of the tail are controlled by muscles so that they can be closed when the bird is at rest, or spread as desired for flight. They, too, have upper and under tail coverts. The tail gives direction in flight, like a rudder, and is used for braking.

The feathers of the wings, tail and body carry the markings and colours of the bird, and all are replaced after moulting by new ones identical in shape and type.

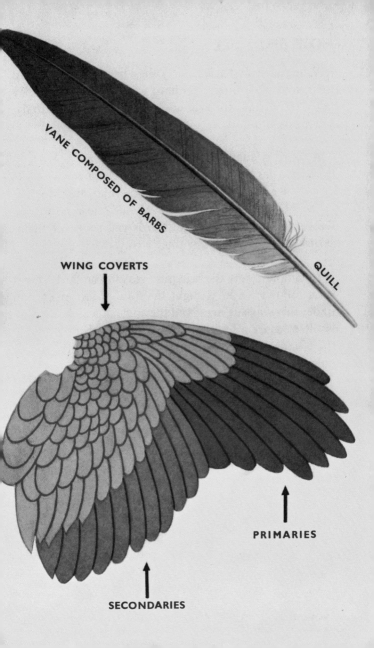

VANE COMPOSED OF BARBS

QUILL

WING COVERTS

PRIMARIES

SECONDARIES

HOW BIRDS FLY

When men first tried to fly they fixed large wings to their arms and flapped as hard as they could, but they could never leave the ground. Man is not designed to fly, but birds are.

A bird is incredibly light for its size. A sea-gull is quite a large bird but it only weighs a few ounces. Many of a bird's bones are hollow and are designed to be both light and strong. We all know how light feathers are. Being so light, birds can soon lift themselves into the air using their strong wing muscles.

In simple terms the scientific reason for birds' flight is as follows: in level flight the flow of air over and under the wing surfaces, and the angle at which the wing is tilted, cause a lower pressure to exist *above* the wing than under it. This gives what is called 'lift', which balances the weight of the bird.

The effect is the same whether the bird is forcing its way through the air or just letting the air pass over its extended wings—as it does when soaring in the wind or circling upward on a rising current of air. When a bird wants to dive fast it folds back its wings, so losing all 'lift', and its own weight takes it rapidly down.

A bird provides power to fly forward by flapping its wings, as explained on page 30, but whenever it can it soars or glides, using the 'lift' provided by its specially shaped wings.

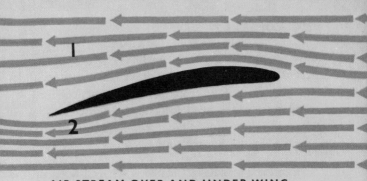

AIR STREAM OVER AND UNDER WING

1 REDUCED
AIR PRESSURE

2 INCREASED
AIR PRESSURE

LEGS AND FEET

Just as the wings of birds have been evolved for different kinds of flight, so have their other limbs developed in different ways. Birds which feed by wading into water need long legs, so the families of waders and shore-birds have long legs; other striking examples are the herons and storks.

Swimming birds have their legs set well back on the body, which is a help when diving and swimming under water. The grebe is a good example; it has the legs it needs to survive.

Feet have also evolved to fit different ways of life. The toes of swans and ducks are joined with flesh to make webbed feet which act as paddles. The coot, another swimmer, has lobes of flesh on its toes for the same reason.

Birds which perch have one strong claw at the back for grasping a branch or twig. A bird that walks or runs has long toes in front and behind, and if, like the hen, it scrapes the ground for its food, the nails grow into the right shape for scraping.

Eagles, vultures and other birds of prey grow very sharp hooked claws, or talons, for seizing their victims. Climbing birds, like the woodpecker, have two toes in front and two behind, to give a good climbing grip.

Perhaps the daintiest claws of all belong to the jacana, or 'lily-trotter'. They are long and slender for walking on floating water plants.

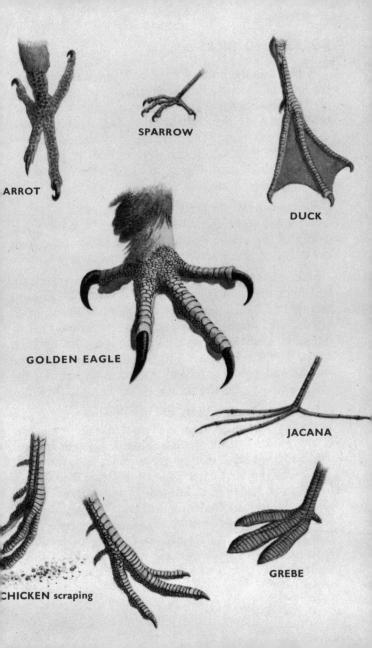

PARROT

SPARROW

DUCK

GOLDEN EAGLE

JACANA

CHICKEN scraping

GREBE

BEAKS AND BILLS

A bird has the kind of beak best suited to deal with the kind of food it eats. Birds which feed on a variety of food have what we might call a 'general purpose' beak. The song thrush is an example; it eats worms, slugs, snails, insects and berries, so it has a medium-sized sharp beak which can deal with all its diet. It is this bird which holds a snail in its beak and cracks the shell against a stone.

Birds such as the large finch family, which live on seeds, have short thick beaks for breaking the outer casing of the seeds. The herons and storks have long beaks for reaching down into the water or mud.

Ducks have wide flat bills to scoop up water or mud and filter the food from it. The edges of the bill have tiny plates called lamellae, through which water is filtered out. Many herons and some ducks have serrations like a saw on their bills for holding the fish they catch. The fish is tossed into the air so that it can be caught and swallowed head-first, thus preventing the scales catching on the inside of the heron's throat.

Eagles and other birds of prey have short, strong beaks for tearing flesh, and the parrot's is like a pair of nut-crackers, and is specially hinged. The woodpecker uses its sharp beak like an axe to dig a hole in a tree. The humming bird has a very slender and delicate bill for sucking nectar from flowers. The very large, strong bill of the toucan enables it to thrust its way through thick foliage to get fruit, and the pelican has a loose pouch which it can fill with fish from a shoal. If you look at a bird's beak you can tell the kind of life it leads and what sort of food it eats.

BULLFINCH

GOLDEN EAGLE

PARROT

THRUSH

WOODPECKER

MALLARD DRAKE

TOUCAN

EYES AND EARS

Birds need sharp sight and hearing to be on the alert for enemies and to help find their food. Hunting birds have the sharpest sight of all. An eagle or a hawk can detect the slightest movement on the ground when it is flying high, and keep the victim in sight as it swoops down to seize it.

Water birds have eyes specially adapted for seeing through and under water, in spite of the refraction of light caused by water. A good example is the kingfisher, which can see a fish while looking into the water, and can still see it after diving to catch it.

Most birds have their eyes on the sides of the head, so that they can see a movement anywhere round them without having to turn the head to look. Birds which hunt large prey are exceptions; they have their eyes in front, as we do. An owl's eyes are very large, almost as big as a man's.

Birds can recognize colours. Sparrows often attack yellow flowers in preference to other colours. A robin in early spring will attack a dummy of red cloth placed near its own haunts, but will ignore a similar dummy of grey cloth.

Birds have no external ears; the 'ears' of the long-eared owl are only tufts of feathers. But they have very sharp hearing. You can see a thrush listening as he hops about a lawn, and when he hears a worm in the ground he will soon pull it out. You try listening for worms in the ground!

NG-EARED OWL

RUSH listening

PRIVATE—KEEP OUT

The robin described on the previous page is not just an aggressive or a bad-tempered bird: it attacks the piece of red cloth because it thinks another robin is invading its own private territory. Robins, and many other kinds of bird, claim an area around their nests as their own private property, and defend it with beak and claw from any other bird of the same species.

The territory claimed is often large enough to provide sufficient food for the bird, its mate and their family; they can then be reasonably sure of survival. Moreover by having their own territory the bird and its mate can usually find food for their young without having to fly too far from the nest. This is important because young birds need a lot of food and the parents have to work very hard to feed them.

When we hear a beautiful bird song we might think it just means that the bird is singing because it is so happy. It may be happy, but that is not why it is singing. The lovely, liquid notes of the blackbird, the haunting song of the nightingale, or the music of the lark as it hovers over a field, are public announcements to all other males of the same species that the particular area has been claimed, is private and that they must keep out. The cock crowing proudly in a farmyard has the same purpose; it announces to all other cocks that the farmyard is his and the hens are his wives, — private, keep out!

ROBIN

COURTSHIP AND DISPLAY

In most species of birds the male has brighter feathers than the female. The male blackbird has jet black feathers and a smart yellow beak, while the female has inconspicuous brown feathers and beak. A cock pheasant is splendid in bright shining feathers while the hen is a smaller, modest, brown bird. Nearly all males grow brighter feathers in the spring, when they want to impress a female and to mate and raise a family.

A cock bird often makes a special display of his feathers to impress a hen. The peacock will spread his great train, all coloured and spotted, and strut up and down in front of the peahen, rattling his fine feathers; he is saying, 'Look what a fine handsome chap I am, how about me for a husband?' Birds of paradise, which are brilliantly coloured, go through an astonishing routine of display. To a lesser degree nearly all male birds display their feathers and colours to the best advantage when they are courting.

When the male and female are of the same colour they often take part in a complicated ritual dance when they are courting, and the dance is always the same in a species. Great crested grebes have a delightful mutual display routine. They shake heads at each other, the male dives and pops up in front of the female who displays her head feathers, and they both dive at the same time and come up together with pieces of weed in their beaks which they offer to each other. Other species of birds have their own particular methods of courting.

PEACOCK displaying

EAT CRESTED GREBES courting

NEST BUILDING

When a pair of birds have mated they need to make a home. In the early spring we have all seen garden birds flying about busily with twigs, pieces of grass and other nest-building materials in their beaks.

There is great variety in the methods and styles of nest-building, but every bird builds only the sort of nest which is typical of its species. Some are miraculously complicated, a good example being that of the long-tailed tit, which makes a domed nest (with an entrance at the side) with moss, lichens, scraps of wool and pieces of spider's web, and lines it with feathers. At the other extreme is the plover, which is content to lay its eggs in a slight hollow in the middle of a field.

Most of the perching birds, sparrows, chaffinches, blackbirds, thrushes, robins, warblers and crows build in trees or hedges, with twigs and grass. Swallows build on ledges, sometimes under the roof of a house, and house martins build rounded nests with small entrance-holes under house eaves. Swallows use mud, grass and hair cemented with saliva, and the house martin uses mud.

Woodpeckers use their strong beaks to make nesting holes in trees. Water birds use reeds or sticks, and sea birds are often content with a ledge on a cliff.

Each species of bird knows by instinct how to build its special kind of nest. Birds which have been kept caged for four generations and then been set free, have built the usual nest of their species, even though they have never previously seen one.

HOUSE MARTIN
and nest

LONG-TAILED TIT
and nest

MALLARD (female)
and nest

EGGS AND HATCHING

When the nest is built the hen bird lays the eggs and a new family is begun. A bird's egg is another of the wonders of creation which we are always finding in the life of birds. Enclosed in the shell is the embryo which grows into the new bird; this embryo is attached to the yolk which provides its food, and both are protected by the 'white'.

The clutch or set of eggs laid by birds varies, and is probably determined by the number of young which the parents can raise. Game birds like the partridge lay up to twenty eggs, while many sea-birds lay only one. Many small perching birds lay four to six eggs and the young fill the nest before they fledge.

Eggs laid in the open are usually specially marked to blend with the surroundings; the lapwing's egg is an example. Eggs laid in nests where the light is dim are often shining white. Shapes of eggs vary; the guillemot's egg is laid on a high cliff ledge and is pointed at one end. If knocked it will roll round, and not over the edge.

Eggs are kept at the correct temperature by the bird sitting on the clutch, turning the eggs from time to time. Garden birds take about thirteen days to hatch their egg, and the cassowary takes eight weeks. When the chick is ready it breaks the shell with its beak, having a special hard piece for the purpose which drops off afterwards. When the shell is broken the chick emerges, a brand new bird.

WING

DUNNOCK

LLEMOT

GOLDEN EAGLE

R DUCK

PARTRIDGE

FAMILY LIFE

When the chicks are hatched the busiest time of the year begins for the parents. The helpless, naked babies, with skinny bodies and large mouths always open for food, keep both parents busy fetching food from morning to night. Young chicks have astonishing appetites; a young finch, for example, eats its own weight in insects every day. It is interesting that finches, rooks and sparrows, which live mainly on seeds, feed their young with insects which are easier to digest. Young pigeons put their beaks inside their parent's beak to get the 'milk' secreted there.

As well as feeding their family, the parent birds have to keep careful guard and clean out the nest—about which they are most particular. By the time the chicks have grown their body feathers and wings, and are ready to fly, the parents are almost worn out with work, and look it! They need the new feathers they grow after they moult.

Not all birds come naked and helpless from the egg. Chickens, goslings and ducklings, for instance, are hatched with their down feathers complete, often bright yellow, and can run about—but always close to their parent hens, geese or ducks. Moorhen chicks are hatched at the water's edge and they, too, are fully clad with down. They go straight from the egg to the water where they float and paddle about happily. Baby cygnets are hatched ready to swim, with pretty grey down and small swan-feet. They spend a lot of time sitting on the parent swan's back as it cruises proudly along.

HAFFINCH
and young

SWAN with cygnets

FOOD AND FEEDING

Some species of birds are vegetarian, others are carnivorous, or meat-eating. The vegetarians live on such things as seeds, fruit, buds and leaves, and the carnivores eat small mammals, fish, snails, reptiles, insects and worms. Birds of prey eat other birds as well as animals. There are also many species which eat both kinds of food, the raven enjoying fruit and grain as well as small animals, eggs and worms.

Swallows and swifts catch insects on the wing. Water birds find their food in the ponds, rivers and sea where they live. A kingfisher, for example, eats water insects, fish, shellfish and tadpoles. Birds which fish in the sea use various methods; the osprey hovers to grab a fish in its talons, a herring gull swoops to catch a fish in its bill and a gannet dives from a height to catch a fish under water.

Birds do not have teeth, but their strong bills are used instead. The seed-eaters also pick up grit needed to grind, in their gizzards, the seeds they have eaten.

The insect-eaters perform a valuable service to mankind, for without them the insects might multiply so fast that many areas would be uninhabitable. Birds which eat seed often drop some of them, and these frequently germinate.

Birds vary in their intelligence and ability to take advantage of new sources of food. If their favourite food is not available in one place, the power of flight enables them to search elsewhere. To us the little tits seem clever and enterprising, because they can solve simple problems and have learned to open the tops of milk bottles.

SWALLOW

RAVEN

KINGFISHER

BLUE TIT

DIFFERENT KINDS OF FLIGHT

Birds have evolved the wings best suited to their particular way of life. For fast flying, long pointed wings are necessary. Look at the wings of the swift in the picture, a bird which can fly at a hundred miles an hour, climb to nine thousand feet, and is even thought to sleep on the wing.

Strong broad wings are best for quick manoeuvring in the air, so hawks, which are hunters, have wings which enable them to turn and twist in the air as they watch their prey on the ground, and then to swoop down on it.

For flapping flight a bird needs fairly small wings which it can move quickly. The wings are moved rapidly upwards and slowly downwards in a screwing motion not unlike a propeller. Another method of flight is to hover, and for this small wings which can be moved very rapidly are required. A humming bird's wings move two hundred times a second, faster than the human eye can see, as it hangs suspended in the air.

Very long wings are needed for soaring flight. The greatest soaring bird is the albatross, which has a wing span of eleven feet. It can fly tirelessly over the sea, wings outstretched, dipping and soaring for hundreds of miles. The eagle is another magnificent flier, soaring for hours with its great wings outstretched. The condor of the high Andes in South America is another wonderful soaring bird. Vultures have a similar wing construction for circling and gliding effortlessly, with wings spread, as they search for their food.

ALBATROSS

SWIFT

HUMMING BIRD

FLIGHTLESS BIRDS

The limbs, organs and faculties a creature needs have been developed during the processes of evolution; other parts gradually become smaller or even disappear. These processes take immensely long periods of time; evolution is reckoned in millions of years.

The ostrich of South Africa has long and powerful legs which have been evolved during its life as a fast-running bird; its wings have become small and useless. Another peculiarity of the ostrich is that it has only two toes instead of the four usual in birds. Because it only runs on one of these, the other is smaller.

The ostrich is the largest of all birds, standing eight feet high and weighing up to three hundred pounds. Other members of the ostrich family, all with small and useless wings and long legs, are the rhea of South America, the cassowary and the emu of Australasia. The smaller kiwis of New Zealand are also flightless.

Another non-flying bird is the penguin, which lives in the coldest parts of the southern hemisphere. Penguins are fine swimmers and live on fish, so their wings have become flippers for swimming. The largest are the Emperor penguins, which live far inside the Antarctic. They stand three feet tall and weigh up to ninety pounds. The smart black and white feathers, the upright stance and the engaging ways of these birds, whether Emperor, King or the little Adelie penguins, make then interesting and attractive to watch.

PENGUIN

OSTRICH

WATER BIRDS AND WADERS

The many species of birds which live on water have adapted themselves accordingly. A swan has webbed feet to act as paddles, a long neck for plunging into the water to get food, and a broad flattened bill for scooping up food in mud or water. The mud or water is then filtered from the beak. Ducks also have broad flat bills and webbed feet. Birds which dive for their food have their legs set well back, which helps both diving and swimming under water.

Water birds are always wonderful swimmers and divers, but they are usually heavy fliers and poor walkers; we have all seen ducks waddling along. However, shags, guillemots and cormorants are all excellent divers, swimmers *and* fliers. Penguins cannot fly at all but they walk well and swim superbly.

Many species of birds wade in water to get their food, and live on the banks of lakes and streams or by the sea. Long legs and beaks are essential for their kind of life. The heron is a typical wader with long legs and a long sword-like beak for catching fish. The curlew has a long bill for probing in the mud for shellfish; this bill is turned down at the end. The avocet's bill is turned up, so that as it wades it can sweep the surface film of water to get its particular kind of food.

Some waders, like the plovers, have short beaks because they feed on fields or by the shore above the water's edge, picking up insects or other small animals that live near or on the ground.

CURLEW

AVOCET

HERON

SEA BIRDS

The best known sea birds are the gulls, which are a common sight wheeling and screaming by the sea shore. There are a number of different kinds of gull, all splendid fliers, and equally at home on sea or land. But gulls are only a group of species in the great number of sea birds.

The terns are graceful birds with long pointed wings and forked tails—which is why they are sometimes called 'sea swallows'. They are wonderful fliers. The best diver of all is the gannet, a large bird with a six foot wing-span. It has special air pockets between skin and body, connected to its lungs, to break the shock of its plummet-like dives into the sea from a height. It attains speeds of up to one hundred and fifty miles an hour on these dives.

The cormorant flies low over the water to dive after fish, overtaking them under water. Skuas have a peculiar way of getting food. They are as big as the gulls which, as well as the smaller terns, they chase until they disgorge their last meal. The skuas then swoop to catch the meal before it reaches the sea.

Guillemots, razorbills and puffins live most of their time on or under the sea. The puffin is also called the 'sea parrot' because of its gaily striped bill of red, blue and yellow.

Petrels only go ashore for short periods in the breeding season; they spend the rest of their time at sea, far out of sight of land. The albatross and the frigate bird are the greatest ocean fliers. They fly immense distances over the open ocean and far from land.

HERRING GULL

GANNET diving

PUFFIN

SOME STRANGE HABITS

The instinct which makes a hen cuckoo lay her eggs in other birds' nests is a mystery which many naturalists have studied. It is a very strange habit. The cuckoo selects some other bird's nest and lays an egg in it, after which she takes no interest at all in the egg. The unsuspecting owners of the nest sit on the egg with their own and hatch it.

When the cuckoo chick emerges it wriggles about in the nest, works its specially hollowed back under the other eggs or chicks, and heaves each one out of the nest until it is the sole occupant.

The foster parents then begin to feed it, and for twenty days they work unceasingly to satisfy the hunger of the outsize chick, for it is always much larger than the real chicks would have been. Even when the young cuckoo is old enough to leave the nest the foster parents still look after it, perching on its back to feed it.

The male bower bird of Australia and New Guinea has a unique way of courting. He builds an elaborate construction of plants and decorates this with brightly coloured objects. When it is finished he displays his feathers and sings in it to the female, to win her. When they do mate they build an ordinary nest for their eggs.

The brush-turkey of Australia and the Pacific lands hatches her eggs in a strange way. The eggs are very large, and they are buried in rotting vegetation, to provide the heat to hatch them. When the chicks emerge they are fully developed and can fly and find their own food. Parents and chicks never meet.

BOWER BIRD
(CRESTLESS GARDENER)

REED WARBLER
ND CUCKOO CHICK

SONG BIRDS

The large group of birds known generally as 'song birds' are those perching birds whose songs appeal to us as being most musical. Birds charm us in many ways, and not least by their glorious music.

It is an exciting experience to hear the 'dawn chorus'. You have to get up *very* early on a fine morning in early summer, while it is still dark, and go to a wood, a park or a garden where there are plenty of trees. Before dawn breaks one or two birds begin to sing, and soon others wake up and join in so that the chorus swells and echoes among the trees. The whole world seems to be full of the loveliest music. It is an experience you will never forget, but it only lasts a few minutes.

The most famous songster is, of course, the nightingale with its song of deep full notes and lovely trills, a wonderful, sustained song. The nightingale sings in the daytime as well as at night.

Blackbird and thrush have rich melodious songs, the linnet's is sweet and varied, the little wren has a remarkably loud, clear song for so small a bird, and the robin's is high and clear. The robin is one of the birds which has a winter song as well, quieter and a little sad. The song of the skylark as the bird sings on the wing is very sweet and thrilling. We all know what a fine songster the canary is.

There is a great number of songbirds, each with its own distinct song, which you can soon learn to recognise. We are fortunate that Britain has so many of them.

MALE AND FEMALE BLACKBIRD

BIRD VOICES

It is not only the 'song birds' which sing; there are other bird songs which may not appeal to the human ear as being musical, but which are songs just the same. The cuckoo's monotonous two notes are its song, and one is always excited to hear the first cuckoo of the year, for this means that spring has come.

The cawing of rooks wheeling about the tall tree-tops is a song. So is the quacking of ducks and the scream of the swift in flight. The cry of sea-birds is as much part of the sea-side as the smell of sea-weed.

Birds 'talk' to each other, especially parent birds to their young. You can hear this if you are near a rookery when there are young, or when a hen clucks softly to her chicks. If you stand near a nest of baby birds you can hear a soft high-pitched twittering.

Some birds use their voices to imitate other creatures. The Australian lyre-bird can make the call or song of any other bird, so realistically that you cannot tell the difference. The most famous mimic is the parrot, which becomes completely tame and can imitate the human voice. Tame budgerigars can be eloquent talkers, too. Other good mimics are the Indian mynah, and the British jackdaw, jay, raven and starling. The starling is a natural mimic, and will imitate all sorts of sounds, perhaps dripping water, a motor car or the calls of other birds.

YELLOW HEADED AMAZON PARROT

BIRD MIGRATION

When we hear the first chiffchaff or see the first swallow or sand martin, we know that winter is over and spring has come. These are some of the large number of birds called *migrants*, birds which have two homes and only come to Britain for the summer. There are also migrants which come for the winter and fly away in the spring; these include the redwing, fieldfare and several kinds of wild geese.

Swallows and storks have been known to fly six thousand miles from northern Europe to South Africa. The wonder is that birds can fly so far and find their destination accurately, for they often return to the previous years' nesting site.

Summer migrants raise their families here, and in the late summer or autumn—sometimes separately, sometimes in families or flocks—they begin the long journey to their other home. When that happens we know that soon winter will come, and we shall have only our own native birds and the winter migrants.

Migrations are usually made in a general north-south direction. Do the birds navigate by the sun and stars across the open ocean? Do they migrate in search of the insects on which many depend? How do they find an exact site, perhaps a farmyard, after flying thousands of miles? Scientists have long studied bird migration, but the full answer to the great mystery is not known. And how do homing pigeons, released up to five hundred miles from their home, find their way unerringly to their own pigeon loft?

SWALLOWS
iving on South Coast

PROTECTION AGAINST ENEMIES

A bird's first defence against an enemy is its sharp sight and hearing, and its ability to fly from danger. Another protection is the colouring of its feathers, which in many cases helps the bird to blend into its surroundings if it stays still. The partridge is an example of protective colouring, and most birds which nest on the ground match their environment. Often the cock bird is brightly coloured while the hen, which has to sit on eggs, is inconspicuously marked.

Another safety precaution used by some species is to move about in large flocks in the winter, when any single bird can give a warning of danger to all the others. Rooks feed together in flocks, and so do starlings and partridges. Starlings also sleep in company. Some roosts are estimated to hold over a million birds, which fly in for many miles from their feeding grounds at dusk.

Birds use tricks to delude an enemy. If a bittern is alarmed on its nest it will point its long bill upwards and stretch its neck to look like the reeds around it. Birds with nests on the ground, such as the skylark and woodcock, will keep quite still when in danger and hope that their protective colouring will prevent them from being seen.

Young birds instinctively stay absolutely still when warned by a parent. Some parent birds will run about dragging a wing, as if it were broken, to draw the enemy away from the nest. Birds even feign death, lying limp and still, with wings slack, to try to trick an enemy.

BITTERN alarmed on its nest

ORNITHOLOGY

Ornithology is the study of the nature and habits of birds, and it is to the work of the ornithologists, and the books they have written, that we owe our knowledge of birds. Work is constantly being done to discover more about birds. To take one example only, a great deal of study is being made of bird migration.

Wild birds are caught, painlessly, in traps, and a small ring bearing a number is gently put round one leg. The bird is then released. If it is caught, perhaps in Africa, the ring is examined and the number noted. This number, and the time and place the bird was caught, are sent to the Natural History department of the British Museum, and the journey the bird made is thus known. When this is done with a great many birds over a long time, information is gained on the migratory habits of a particular species.

There are bird observation stations at selected places, and bird sanctuaries where wild birds can be safe and breed undisturbed. Special studies are made at establishments such as the Wildfowl Trust in Gloucestershire, where geese and duck are studied.

In Britain all wild birds are protected by law, except a few 'pest' species like the woodpigeon, and it is an offence, punishable by a fine, to kill them or take their eggs. Some species of wild birds have become extinct in the past because people destroyed them, perhaps for sport, perhaps for some commercial reason. A recent example is the osprey, which has only just begun to breed again in Britain, and is now very carefully protected.

DETACHABLE
NET

SCREENS FOR
DECOYMAN

DECOY
ENTRANCE

WIREMESH

SCREEN FOR
DECOYMAN

BAIT

CORNER OF POND

RINGING
MALLARD (male)

BIRD WATCHING

You can recognise a particular bird in several ways: by its plumage, by its flight, by its song or call or by its nest. Recognition of birds is a never-failing source of delight, and sooner or later you have the thrill of seeing a really rare bird. Bird watching is a hobby anyone can have.

Many books are available, from very beautiful and expensive ones to reliable and inexpensive paper-backs, and all will give you information, about species, markings, habits, breeding and song. First you will get to know the different species, and there are many indeed in Britain, and then the different members of each species. For example, twelve species of warbler, five owls and six gulls breed in Britain.

Your knowledge will quickly increase as you watch the birds. You need basic knowledge and patience, and you will probably want to make a 'hide'. You must learn to keep quite still for a long time; it is always rewarding. Write what you see in a notebook, noting the date, the Greenwich Mean Time, the weather and the wind direction. There will probably be a natural history or an ornithological society in your district which you can join.

Britain is blessed with a great wealth of wild birds, thanks to her trees, hedges and fields, her rivers and lakes, her cliffs and beaches on the coast, and her climate. In the life of wild birds, their flight, their songs and calls, their colour and every aspect of their busy, clever lives, there is constant delight for anyone who knows how to watch them.

A LIST OF BIRDS

These are some of the many different species of birds.
Numbers indicate pages where they are mentioned.
Heavy type indicates a picture.